STOLEN HEART

STOLEN HEART

TALES OF ELTHERA: A PREQUEL

KAELIS KNIGHT

PUBLISHED BY EVERSPELL MEDIA

www.kaelisknight.com

Copyright © 2025 by Kaelis Knight

Cover Design & Art: Everspell Media

ISBN: 978-1-7644694-1-8 (Paperback)

ISBN: 978-1-7644694-0-1 (Ebook)

First Edition: December 2025

9 8 7 6 5 4 3 2

Printed in the country of purchase

For Lena.

*For your fierce heart, and your unshakeable belief
that love is always worth fighting for.*

CONTENT NOTE

Stolen Heart is a prequel novella intended for adult audiences. It contains mature themes, including:

- Explicit sexual content
- Discrimination and classism (Fantasy racism against magic users)
- Depictions of poverty, starvation, and homelessness
- Medical distress (A child with severe illness)
- Trauma and kidnapping themes

Please Note:

As a prequel to the *Tales of Elthera*, this novella serves as an origin story and ends on a **dramatic cliffhanger.** The saga continues in *Silent Heart*, where a new romance takes center stage and Dave and Lena's ultimate fate is revealed—happily ever after guaranteed.

For a detailed list of specific content warnings, please visit:
kaelisknight.com/content-warnings

Table of Contents

THE KINGDOM OF ELTHERA

NORTHERN REACHES

GREYPORT

WIDE SEA

WESTERN PLANES

EASTERN TERRITORIES

CAPITAL

RESIDENCE OF THE KING

SERPENT'S PASSAGE

THE FREE ISLES

N
W E
S

CHAPTER 1

Lena sat huddled against the wall of a dark alley, snow banking against her shins. She didn't feel the cold. With the flame that lived inside her, a constant ember burning low in her chest, no winter could touch her. It was the one consolation she had left.

She held a hand before her face and watched the fire flicker in her palm, golden and warm without burning, the only thing distracting her from the cramp in her stomach.

Three weeks since she'd last had a proper meal, since Lord Barclay had shoved her through the manor gates into Greyport's bitter winter.

"You're free to go," the young lord had said, thrusting the papers at her chest. "Father's sentimentality ends with his corpse."

Ten years she had served his father. "My little flame," the old lord used to call her, as if she were a candle to be lit and snuffed at his pleasure. A decade of stoking fires and heating baths, of being property after her parents—poor farmers with too many mouths to feed—had sold her the day she turned twelve, the age at which all magic users were required to be registered.

Now, at twenty-two, she owned nothing but the clothes on her back and a piece of paper that proclaimed her free. She had read the words so many times they were seared into her memory:

Be it known that the magic user identified as Leonora Willoughby, designated as Fire Starter, is hereby released from bondage under the Protection of the Realm Act, Section 7, Clause 3: Voluntary Manumission by Master's Heir. Said individual is granted permission to exist freely within the kingdom's borders, subject to all restrictions and limitations prescribed by law for persons of magical designation.

Finally, after so many years of dreaming about it, she was free.

Free to starve.

She had drifted deeper into the city these past weeks, into the Warrens. That labyrinth of cramped alleys where the desperate made their homes and magic users who had slipped through the cracks eked out miserable existences in the shadows. She had tried to find work, but one look at her eyes, the faint spectral glow that marked her kind, and doors slammed in her face.

"We don't hire Sparks."

"You demons aren't welcome here."

So she had found this alley between two crumbling buildings, narrow enough that unsuspecting passersby wouldn't notice her. At least she would never freeze. She could sleep in snowdrifts while others died of cold.

But fire couldn't fill an empty stomach.

Her gut twisted as she watched the flame dance in her palm, letting it pull her thoughts away from the gnawing pain—

"Spark-rat!"

The shout ripped through the darkness, and Lena's head snapped up to find a man standing at the entrance of the alley, middle-aged, heavyset, his lip curled back to show yellowed teeth. His clothes were rough, caked with mud, his hands balled into fists.

"Disgusting creature!" He spat, the glob of saliva landing inches from her feet. "Using your devil's fire in the open like you own the bloody streets!"

The small flame in her palm guttered and died.

Lena met the man's eyes without flinching.

She could kill him. One targeted blast of her fire would reduce this fool to ash before he could scream.

"I wasn't hurting anyone," she said flatly. "I was just keeping myself warm."

"And cursing us all with your unnatural ways?" The brute took a step into the alley, and Lena saw others gathering behind him. A woman with hard eyes, and two younger men who looked eager for violence. "Creatures like you should be collared and kenneled, not walking free among God-fearing men."

"I have papers." She rose, her back against the wall, her hands loose at her sides. Ready. "I'm legally freed. I'm not breaking any laws."

"Papers." The man laughed, a phlegmy, ugly sound. "Hear that, lads? The Spark-rat has papers." He cracked his knuckles. "Papers don't mean a damn thing in the Warrens, love. Not when you're sitting in our alley, stinking up our air with your cursed magic."

Heat prickled in her palms. Her fire rose, responding to the fury building in her chest.

She knew what would happen if she unleashed it. The law held no mercy for magic users who harmed ordinary citizens, even in self-defense. She would hang before the week was out, strung up without trial.

But three weeks of starvation and cruelty had worn her down. She was done being afraid.

Let them burn, the fire whispered. Let them all burn.

The man reached for her—

And Lena's control snapped.

Fire roared up her arms, licking at her sleeves, her eyes blazing like hot coals. For one beat, she didn't care about the consequences. Didn't care about the magistrates or the noose.

Do it. Show them what a Spark-rat can really do.

"That's quite enough."

The voice that came from behind the crowd was calm and carried an authority that made everyone pause. Even Lena.

The fire died in her hands. She stood there, shaking. Her palms still smoked, and the brute's hand hovered inches from her arm, frozen mid-reach.

Dear Lord. The adrenaline crashed, leaving cold horror in its wake. *I almost—I nearly—*

The crowd parted, and a man emerged from the darkness.

He was younger than she'd expected from the weight in his voice. Perhaps twenty-five. Tall and broad-shouldered, with sandy hair cropped short. He moved confidently, like a man who rarely spoke twice, yet he lacked the sneer of the aristocracy. His clothes were simple wool, well-made but darning stitches marked the cuffs.

What caught her attention most of all though was his face. He was handsome, undeniably so, but he looked wrecked. Deep, bruised circles darkened the skin beneath his brown eyes, and his complexion was gray, as if he hadn't slept in a week.

When he stepped closer, she thought she saw a faint shimmer in his irises, there and gone.

"Who the bloody hell are you?" the man next to her demanded.

"Someone who doesn't appreciate mobs cornering defenseless women." The stranger's gaze swept over the gathered people, cool and assessing, lingering on Lena's still-smoking palms before settling on her face. His brow furrowed. "This woman has committed no crime. I suggest you find somewhere else to be."

"Mind your own affairs, stranger. This don't concern you."

"It concerns me now." His tone sharpened. "Under the Protection of the Realm Act of 1847, harassment of freed magic users carries a penalty of ten silver coins. I'd be happy to escort the gentleman to the nearest magistrate if he'd like to test that."

For a moment, no one moved. Then the woman with the hard eyes tugged at the brute's sleeve.

"Leave it, Jasper. She ain't worth the trouble."

Jasper glared at the stranger, then spat again and jerked his head toward the alley's exit. "Come on, then. Let the Spark-lover have his pet."

They shuffled back into the depths of the Warrens, muttering curses. Snow began to fall, heavy flakes drifting down. Lena stayed pressed against the wall, adrenaline fading, the crushing weight of three weeks' starvation threatening to fold her knees.

The stranger stepped toward her, slow and deliberate, the way one approaches a wild animal. This near, she got a better look at him. His eyes weren't just brown; they were the color of old whiskey held up to the light, studying her with absolute focus.

"You're shaking," Dave said, keeping his voice soft, unthreatening. Up close, he could see how thin she was. Her cheekbones stood out sharp beneath the pale skin. Dark hair fell in tangled strands around a face that was striking despite the gauntness. She had full lips and eyes that burned with amber fire—even now, exhausted and half-starved.

"Are you hurt?" he asked.

She shook her head, then immediately swayed, her hand flying to the wall for balance. Her eyes lost focus, and Dave lunged forward before she could fall.

"Easy." He caught her arm, steadying her. God, she weighed nothing. "Can you stand?"

She tried, he had to give her credit for that. She straightened her spine, squared her shoulders, and attempted to push away from the wall. But her legs buckled, and she collapsed backward.

Dave caught her without hesitation, one arm wrapping around her waist to hold her upright. She stiffened at the contact, and he made sure his grip was gentle, careful not to bruise the too-thin arms beneath his hands.

"I've got you," he said softly, shifting to take more of her weight. She was light enough that he could have carried her outright, but something told him she would hate that. "I know a place where we can get you food and a bed for the night."

Her head snapped up, her eyes sharp with suspicion.

"You're not taking me to a church, are you?" The words came out with surprising venom for someone who could barely stand. "You might as well put an end to me right now. Do you know what the clergy does to people like me?"

Dave laughed, surprising himself with the sound. "No church," he assured her. "They wouldn't have you, and we both know it. I'm taking you somewhere your fire will be welcome, not condemned."

She went still in his arms, searching his face, and Dave felt the weight of her scrutiny. She was looking for the trap, he realized. His chest tightened at what that said about her life, about what she must have endured to make suspicion her first instinct.

"Why?" she asked, her voice barely more than a whisper. "Why help me?"

It was a fair question. One he'd asked himself a thousand times over the years as he'd ventured into the Warrens. The answer had never changed.

"Because someone has to." He looked down at her. "My name is David. Dave, to my friends. And I promise, where I'm taking you, no one will judge you for what you are."

Her expression wavered, tears gathering at the corners of her eyes, but she swiftly blinked them back.

"My name is Leonora," she managed. "But you may call me Lena."

"Well, Lena." Dave shifted, slinging her arm over his shoulders. Her warmth surprised him. Most people he found on the winter streets were half-frozen. But Lena radiated heat like a banked coal. "Let's get you somewhere safe."

They emerged onto a wider street, still deep in the Warrens but lit by a few sputtering oil lamps. Snow was falling heavier now, thick flakes catching in Lena's dark hair, melting away where they met the heat of her skin. Dave guided her carefully over the uneven cobblestones, adjusting his pace to match her stumbling steps.

"The shelter," she said, "how do you know about it?"

"I run it. Try to keep the larder full and the roof from leaking."

"And you just... wander the streets at night, looking for starving people to rescue?"

Her tone was skeptical, almost mocking. Dave huffed a quiet laugh. He liked that—liked that even now, weak and desperate, she refused to simply accept what he told her.

It was, he thought, probably what had kept her alive this long.

"Not usually," he admitted. "I was on my way back from a meeting with a potential donor who never showed. Took a shortcut on my way back and saw the commotion."

He steered her around a puddle of murky liquid. "The shelter could use an extra pair of hands," he continued. "If you're willing. Once you've recovered, of course."

He felt her stiffen slightly against him.

"I'm a fire starter. Perhaps not what you want in your home. You saw what I nearly did back there."

"That's exactly what we want in our home," he said firmly. "And what matters is that you stopped yourself."

She stumbled, and he caught her, his arm tightening around her waist. He met her gaze, seeing the exhaustion warring with the defiance. Those dark brown eyes seemed to see straight through him.

He wondered if she could see the faint glow in his own eyes; the one thing all magic users had in common. Most people missed it, dismissed it as a trick of the light. But Lena was looking at him now with dawning realization, her lips parting in surprise.

"The shelter serves everyone, Lena. Magic users most of all," he explained, confirming what she had already guessed. "None of us asked for these gifts. The world punishes us for them anyway. The least we can do is look after one another."

He watched her eyes widen with understanding.

"You're a—"

"Enhancer." Dave smiled. "Not much use for starting fires, I'm afraid. But I can keep people alive when everything else fails."

Her mind was working, he could see it, the implications clicking into place.

"How?" she breathed. "How have they not caught you? The Protection of the Realm Act—"

"Doesn't apply to people who've never been recorded." His jaw tightened involuntarily. "I was

13

never on the lists. My gift doesn't show the way other gifts do. And the glow is so faint most people don't even notice it."

"But the shelter... if anyone found out—"

"If they found out, the shelter closes and I disappear." He shrugged. "I know the risks. I choose to take them anyway."

Lena was silent. When he glanced down at her, he could see the question forming in her eyes: *Why?*

But before she could ask, they rounded the final corner, and Haven came into view.

"Here we are."

Lena swayed on her feet as they stopped in front of a large, nondescript building, the windows shuttered tight against the cold. A hand-painted sign above the door read simply: *Haven.*

"It's not much," Dave said, guiding her toward the entrance. "But there's food, and you'll be safe here."

The door swung open before they reached it, revealing a stout woman with gray-streaked hair and kind eyes. She took one look at Lena and swiftly stepped aside.

"Good God, Dave, who have you found this time? The poor girl looks half-starved!" The woman was already hurrying toward a massive fireplace where flames danced high and bright. "Come, come, sit here by the fire. I'll fetch soup and blankets—Mary! Mary, put on more water for tea!"

Lena let herself be guided to a worn but comfortable chair near the hearth. The room was larger than she'd expected. The building had been a warehouse once, or perhaps a granary, now converted into something between a dormitory and a home. Mismatched furniture filled the space: chairs salvaged from better houses, tables scarred by years of use, pallets lined along the far wall where blankets were piled high. The smell of wood smoke and cooking filled the air.

Her mouth watered at the savory scent, but it was the fire that called to her, and she leaned into its warmth instinctively.

"Drink this." The gray-haired woman pressed a steaming bowl into Lena's hands. "Slowly, child. Your stomach's likely not ready for much."

Lena raised the dish to her lips with unsteady hands. The warmth of the broth hit her stomach with a shock, almost painful after so long without food.

Dave crouched beside her chair, watching her closely. "Feel better?"

She nodded, not trusting her voice.

"Good." He reached out and rested his hand on her shoulder. "Rest tonight. Eat. We can talk about what comes next in the morning." He nodded toward the gray-haired woman. "Mrs. Finch will see you have everything you need. Dry clothes, a place to sleep."

"I don't—" The words caught in her throat. "I don't have any way to repay you."

"I'm not asking for payment." He rose, and cold air rushed into the space where his hand had just been.

Lena looked around the room; at the fire crackling in the hearth, at the other people huddled in chairs and on pallets along the walls.

Magic users, she realized. All of them, or most. She could see it in the way they held themselves, the wariness in their eyes, the haunted look of people who had spent their lives being treated as less than human.

And then there was Dave. The man who was risking everything to give them this sanctuary.

A decision took root in her before she'd fully formed the thought. She turned back to find him watching her.

"I'll stay and help," she said, surprising herself with how easily the words came. "If your offer still stands."

CHAPTER 2

"The Hendersons need more blankets," Lena said, consulting the worn ledger in her hands. "And Mr. Carver's cough is getting worse. I think we should move him closer to the hearth."

Dave nodded, dipping his quill into the ink pot, but his eyes drifted past the page. He watched her move through the shelter's main hall, securing a loose shutter against the wind before checking on a sleeping child. She had become indispensable in eight weeks, learning Haven's rhythms as if she'd been born to them. Now she was reaching for a stack of linens before Mrs. Finch had even asked for them.

Outside, a late winter storm battered the walls, piling snow against the doors and making travel through Greyport nearly impossible. The shelter was fuller than Dave had ever seen it.

Every pallet was occupied, every corner claimed by someone seeking refuge from the brutal cold.

And there was Lena, moving through the gloom, a stark contrast to the half-dead woman he'd helped out of that alley two months ago.

Her dark hair, lank and matted that first night, was tied back now, though a few curly strands escaped to frame her face. The hollow gauntness of her cheeks had given way to the flush of exertion. She moved with a strength that had been absent before, shoulders squared, steps silent and sure.

Dave watched her pause by the massive stone hearth, her sharp profile illuminated by the soft glow of the dying fire. She tossed a fresh log onto the grate, yet she didn't reach for the poker to stoke the damp wood. Instead, she simply raised a hand, palm open toward the embers.

He sat motionless, mesmerized as her eyes flared with sudden, molten intensity. The flames leaped in response to her silent calling, roaring back to life, dancing higher to lick at the soot-stained bricks. She wasn't just tending the fire; she was commanding it.

In that moment, backlit by the surge of orange light, she looked terrifying and magnificent all at once.

"Dave? Did you hear what I said?"

He blinked as Lena turned from the hearth and started walking toward him. The fiery glow in her eyes faded back to brown as she approached, stopping in front of his desk with one eyebrow raised.

"Sorry," he said, clearing his throat and looking down at the ink-stained page to hide his embarrassment. "It's loud in here today."

"About Mr. Carver?"

"Yes," he said, grateful for the prompt. "Yes, move him closer to the fire. I'll check on him myself later tonight."

Lena nodded, her gaze lingering on him for a second longer than necessary before she turned back to her work.

Dave let out a slow breath, gripping the quill tight enough to bend the feather. He needed to focus. There were supplies to ration, repairs to schedule, and a dozen new arrivals to vet.

Mrs. Finch passed behind him, arms full of clean linens, and paused just long enough to follow his gaze toward Lena, who was now helping Mr. Carver sit up.

"She keeps the cold out, Dave," the older woman murmured, her voice barely audible against the howling of the wind. "Better than the logs do."

She was gone before Dave could respond, heading toward the sleeping quarters without waiting for an answer.

He looked down at his hands. Mrs. Finch saw too much. But she didn't understand the risk. There was always another mouth to feed, another crisis to manage. He couldn't afford distractions, not when a single slip could bring the Magistrate down on all of them.

Across the room, Lena looked up from where she was adjusting the old man's blankets. Their eyes met across the crowded hall. She offered him a smile. Small, tired, but genuine.

Dave smiled back.

"How do you pay for all this?" Lena asked the next morning, gesturing with her spoon at the hall around them.

Dave looked up from his bowl, surprised. "What do you mean?"

"The food. The coal. The building." She frowned, lowering her voice so the people nearby wouldn't hear. "I've been here two months, and never once have I seen you turn anyone away. You feed them, clothe them, give them beds. But I've also never seen anyone pay a single copper." She met his eyes. "So how does it work?"

Dave shifted on the hard wooden bench, considering how much to tell her. She deserved the truth, she'd more than earned it, but he had given his word.

"The shelter was founded by an anonymous benefactor," he said finally. "Someone wealthy. Someone who understands what people like us go through."

"A noble?"

"I assume so. The funds he supplies each month are substantial. A rich soul with a guilty conscience. Or maybe just a good heart."

Lena looked surprised. "You don't know who it is?"

"I know enough." Dave stirred his porridge. "He's a young lord, from what I can tell. Younger than you'd expect for that kind of coin. Quiet. Intense. He has these eyes, storm gray and sharp as—"

He stopped himself, the description dying in his throat as he realized he was saying too much.

"He values his privacy," Dave finished abruptly. "And I value his gold. We have an understanding."

Lena studied him, but she didn't press. "And the money he sends, it's enough? To keep all this running?" she asked.

"Mostly. The funds cover the building and the essentials—coal, clothing, the bulk of the grain. But for the rest..." He hesitated. "I have to scrape for it. I talk merchants into donating goods before they spoil. I find nobles who want their charity kept off the books. It takes a fair bit of groveling. Trading favors."

"Trading," Lena repeated. "With nobles."

"With anyone willing to pay." Dave's jaw tightened. "It's not always pleasant. Some of them want to feel virtuous without getting their hands dirty. Others want information, introductions, things I can't always provide. But if bowing to self-important lords means the children here don't go hungry, then I bow."

Lena watched him with an intensity that made him feel exposed.

"You carry a great deal," she said softly. "More than one person should."

"It's necessary." His expression darkened, the spoon scraping against the bottom of his bowl. "It's not just the cold I'm trying to save people from, Lena. The streets aren't safe. Not anymore."

She frowned. "What do you mean?"

Dave lowered his voice further, leaning in. "A while ago, I started noticing faces missing. Regulars who come here for a hot meal. People I check on in the alleys. One day they were there, and the next..." He shook his head. "Gone."

"Maybe they moved on? Or the cold took them?"

"I checked. No bodies found. No arrests in the Magistrate's logs."

"Do you have any idea what's happening to them?"

"None. They just vanish."

"All the more reason to look after yourself," she said firmly. "You're no use to anyone if you collapse. Or worse."

Dave forced a smile, though it didn't reach his eyes. "I'm stronger than I look. And the people here need me."

"They need you alive."

The words hung between them, heavy and uncomfortably true.

Dave looked away, focusing on the embers in the hearth. She wasn't wrong. He could feel the strain. The endless effort of holding Haven together with nothing but will and borrowed coin was slowly wearing him down.

But what choice did he have? There was no one else to carry this burden.

"The morning deliveries should arrive soon," he said, rising from the bench. "Would you mind helping Mrs. Finch sort them?"

Lena looked at him as though she had more to say. But then she simply nodded and rose as well.

He watched her walk toward the kitchen, the silence she left behind heavier than the storm howling outside.

The storm had been building all day.

Lena had just returned from her daily rounds through the Warrens, searching for those in need—a task she had taken on because she was the only one who could brave the cold without suffering. She would often leave a little of her fire with those who refused to come inside, warming their hands or their hearths before moving on.

But today had been different. After Dave spoke of the disappearances that morning, she had pushed harder, lingering longer in the streets. Safety in the Warrens was always relative, but the idea that people, magic users most of all, could simply disappear without a trace left her profoundly unsettled. People didn't just vanish into thin air.

Her boots were damp from snow as she made her way to the cooking fires to help prepare supper. She found herself wondering if Dave would join them for dinner tonight. He often forgot to eat when he was busy—and he was always busy. Just the thought of him sent a flutter through her chest, one she had stopped trying to ignore weeks ago.

A clatter from the kitchen cut through the din of the overcrowded hall. Mrs. Finch's voice rang out, calling for more bowls.

Lena quickened her pace. The shelter was bursting at the seams tonight. She took her place at the great pot to help ladle out supper, resolving to make sure Dave ate something before the night was done.

She was just handing a steaming bowl to an elderly man when the front door burst open.

A gust of wind tore through the hall, carrying a swirl of snow that made those closest to the draft cry out and shield their faces. A woman stumbled across the threshold, wild-eyed and frantic. She held a little boy clutched tight against her chest, his face pale and blue-tinged, his small body shaking with violent tremors.

"Please," the woman gasped. "They said you could help. They said there was a healer here—"

Dave appeared from the back corridor, his face grave. "I'm not a healer. But I can try to help. Bring him to the back room." He glanced at Lena, his expression tight. "Come with me, I'll need you."

She set down her ladle and followed as he led the woman through the hall and into a small chamber, Mrs. Finch hurrying after them.

The room was sparse. Just a narrow bed, a washstand, and a single chair. And it was bitterly cold. Before anything else, Lena crossed to the small iron stove in the corner. She grabbed a shovel of coals from the bucket, shoved them inside the grate, and held up her palm. A burst of heat shot from her hand, igniting the coals instantly. She slammed the iron door shut as the fire roared to life.

The mother laid her son on the bed, her hands shaking so badly she could barely let go of him.

"What happened?" Dave asked, two fingers pressed to the boy's neck.

"Consumption," the woman managed. "He's been sick for weeks, but the cold..." She swallowed hard, fighting the tears. "It made every-thing worse. We couldn't reach the doctor in this weather. We barely made it this far." She looked up, desperate. "Please. He's all I have."

Lena felt her heart sink. She had seen consumption before, in Lord Barclay's household. The servants who caught it were discreetly dismissed, sent away to die somewhere that wouldn't inconvenience the family.

"Everyone out," Dave ordered. "Lena, stay."

Mrs. Finch led the sobbing mother out, closing the door behind them.

"He's half-frozen," Dave said, stripping the wet coat from the shivering boy. "My magic won't take until we get some warmth back into him. You have to help him."

Lena nodded and moved to the bedside. She placed her hands on the boy's small chest, feeling his icy skin through the thin shirt. Closing her eyes, she called forth her flame, channeling it through her palms and into the child's frozen body, willing it to spread through his tiny limbs.

Gradually, the blue tinge faded from his lips. His trembling eased. Color began to return to his cheeks, faint, but there.

"That's it," Dave murmured, watching closely. "Good. Keep him steady."

After several minutes, Lena felt the boy's body temperature stabilize. He was still cool, but no longer dangerously cold. She let out a long breath, her shoulders dropping as the tension released.

"I think he's ready," she said.

Dave nodded, rolling up his sleeves.

"This is going to look bad," he warned. "Whatever happens, hold him down."

Lena shifted her grip, moving her hands to the boy's shoulders and stepping to the head of the bed to brace him. Dave stepped into the space she had vacated at the bedside, placing both hands on the boy's chest.

The atmosphere in the room changed.

She felt it before she saw it. A shift in the air, heavy and static, like the moment before a lightning strike. Dave's eyes, normally brown with only the faintest shimmer, flared into a brilliant, burning gold.

The boy gasped. His back arched off the bed, his small hands clutching at the sheets. Lena leaned her weight onto his shoulders, keeping him pinned as he thrashed.

"Hold him," Dave grunted.

Lena watched, transfixed, as the energy poured from him. A visible distortion formed in the air, a transfer of raw force flowing from Dave's hands into the child's small frame.

With each pulse, the boy's breathing eased. The thrashing stopped and the desperate rattling gasps smoothed into a steady rhythm.

But Dave...

Dave was fading.

The color drained from his face, leaving his skin gray and waxy. The shadows under his eyes deepened until they looked like bruises. His hands trembled where they pressed against the boy's chest, and Lena could see the visible toll it was taking to keep the effort up.

"Dave," she said. "Dave, stop. That's enough."

"Almost... there..."

One final pulse of energy, leaving Dave's eyes blazing in a sharp flash. Then the light snapped out, his hands dropped from the boy's chest, and he stumbled backward.

Lena lunged to catch his arm, bracing him before he could hit the floor. He was shaking violently, his breath coming in shallow gasps, his skin clammy and cold beneath her hands. She guided him down to sit against the wall, her heart pounding. He looked aged beyond his years—as if a decade of life had been stripped away in the span of minutes.

"The boy," he managed through chattering teeth. "Is he—"

Lena looked toward the bed. The child was still pale, still sick, but his breathing had steadied. His eyes were closed, his small face peaceful in sleep.

"He's stable," she said. "But Dave, you—"

"I'll recover." He leaned his head back against the wall, his whole body trembling. "Always do. Just... need a moment."

"A moment?" she repeated, unable to keep the edge from her voice. "You nearly killed yourself."

"Didn't, though." A ghost of a smile crossed his gray lips. "Takes more than that to finish me off."

Lena wanted to shake him. She wanted to demand what kind of fool risked his own life so carelessly. But looking at his gray skin and the violent shivers wracking his frame, she realized no warmth remained in him.

She knelt beside him, took his ice-cold hands in hers, and called forth her fire, just as she had done for the boy.

Dave's eyes flew open, the golden shimmer gone, leaving them dark and blown wide. "Lena—"

"Quiet." She tightened her grip on his hand. "You're freezing. Let me help."

He held her gaze, his expression unreadable. Then, slowly, he relaxed against the wall and let her flame seep into him.

She watched as his features softened, the deep lines of exhaustion easing, the gray pallor retreating. The energy of her heat seemed to restore some of the vitality he had given away. Gradually, some color returned to his cheeks. His breathing slowed. The trembling in his limbs eased, though he still looked worn and weary.

"How do you feel?" she asked.

"Better," he said, his voice steadier now. "Thank you."

Lena kept her grip on his fingers, reluctant to let go. The heat between their palms felt suddenly intimate, a stark contrast to the cold room.

"You can't keep doing this," she said, her throat tight. "Giving pieces of yourself away until there's nothing left."

"Someone has to help them."

"Not at the cost of your own life."

Dave's smile was sad. "I happened to be born with this gift." He squeezed her hand. "If I can use it to save a child from dying before his time, then I do it."

Lena wanted to argue. Wanted to tell him that he shouldn't risk his life like that. That he was too important—to Haven, to the people who depended on him. To her. But the words stuck in her throat.

So instead, she helped him to his feet, supporting him when he swayed. Before they left, she unfolded the blanket sitting at the foot of the bed and tucked it securely around the sleeping boy, making sure he was warm. Then she followed Dave out of the small room and back toward the main hall, ready to steady him should his strength fail again.

The mother was waiting by the hearth, her face a mask of desperate hope.

"Your son is stable," Dave told her, and his voice betrayed none of the exhaustion that Lena could see trembling through his limbs. "He should remain so until you can find a doctor, once this storm passes."

The woman burst into tears, clasping Dave's hands in hers, pouring out a flood of gratitude. Lena stood at his side, keeping a protective watch as he silently accepted the praise.

He had nearly killed himself to save that child. And now he stood there, pale and trembling, listening to the woman's thanks as if he'd done nothing more remarkable than lend someone a coin.

You carry a great deal, she had told him.

She hadn't known the half of it.

Later, after the mother and child had been settled in the sleeping quarters, Mrs. Finch insisted that Dave retire to his chamber and rest.

"You've done enough for one night," she said. "Theo will help you upstairs. And you'll eat something substantial before you sleep."

Dave looked ready to protest, but then he seemed to think better of it and allowed Theo, one of the younger volunteers, to guide him toward the stairs, his steps slow and unsteady.

Lena watched him go, the knot in her chest tightening. Outside, the storm continued to rage, wind howling against the shutters, snow piling ever higher against the doors.

Mrs. Finch stepped into the kitchen area and returned a moment later with a bowl of steaming stew.

"Here." She pressed it into Lena's hands. "Would you take this up to him? Make sure he eats every bite. I'm needed down here, and that fool will waste away if someone doesn't look after him."

Lena nodded and climbed the narrow stairs to the upper floor. She had never been to Dave's private chamber before, but Mrs. Finch had given her a task, and she intended to see it through. Besides, she needed to see for herself that he was alright.

The door was slightly ajar. She knocked softly and pushed it open.

The room was small and sparse—a narrow bed against one wall, a washstand in the corner, a small writing desk stacked with neat piles of paper. A tiny iron stove sat dark near the window. Dave lay propped against the pillows, his eyes closed, his face still carrying that weary pallor.

The room was freezing. She could hear the wind battering against the glass, feel the cold seeping through the thin walls.

Lena set the bowl of stew on the desk and crossed to the stove. A few gray embers still glowed faintly in the grate, struggling against the chill. She fed a couple of fresh logs onto the coals and held out her hand. The flames obeyed instantly, radiating heat into the small space.

"You didn't have to do that."

Dave's voice was weak, but he was watching her now, his eyes half-open.

"Your room is ice-cold." Lena retrieved the bowl of stew and brought it to his bedside. "And Mrs. Finch will have my head if you don't eat this."

He made a face, though it lacked any real conviction. "I'm not hungry."

"Please, Dave." She sat on the edge of his bed. "Just a little. You need the strength."

He sighed, his expression weary. But he took the bowl from her hands, and lifted the spoon to his mouth.

She watched him eat as the fire crackled in the stove, slowly warming the room. The food seemed to steady him, settling the tremor in his hands, though the heavy gray pallor of exhaustion didn't leave his face.

"You scared me tonight," she said after a while. "When you collapsed."

Dave paused, the spoon halfway to his mouth. "I'm sorry. I didn't mean to frighten you."

"You pushed yourself too far."

"I did what I had to do."

"I know."

Lena's chest ached. She thought of everything she'd witnessed over the past months—the long hours he worked, the meals he skipped, the way exhaustion shadowed his eyes even on the best days. The way he poured himself into Haven, never asking for anything in return. He was burning himself out. And he didn't seem to realize it.

"Teach me," she said.

Dave blinked, setting the empty bowl aside. "What?"

"Teach me how to help. Not your magic—I know I can't do what you do. But the rest of it. The running of this place." She held his gaze, her voice quiet but firm. "You can't carry it all alone, Dave. Let me help you."

CHAPTER 3

You can't carry it all alone, Dave. Let me help you.

The words hung in the air between them, and Dave felt his defenses crumble.

He had been alone for so long. Even surrounded by volunteers, by the people he helped, by Mrs. Finch's motherly fussing—he had always been solitary in the ways that mattered. The weight of Haven rested on his shoulders. The secrets, the risks, the constant fear of discovery. The knowledge that one wrong move could destroy everything he had built, could condemn everyone who depended on him.

He had never let anyone close enough to share that burden. Had never trusted anyone enough to let them see how heavy it truly was.

Until now.

Until her.

Dave set the bowl of stew aside, his hands trembling. Stabilizing the boy had cost him more than he wanted to admit. His life force was dangerously depleted, his body crying out for rest. Without Lena's warmth earlier, he would have been bedridden for a week at the very least. Even now, he knew he would need days to fully recover.

Maybe the storm was a blessing in disguise. With the city buried under snow, Haven locked tight against the blizzard, he could afford to rest. Just this once.

"Thank you," he said quietly. "Truly, Lena. I don't... I'm not used to..."

A shiver ran through him despite the fire now heating the small room, and he saw her eyes sharpen with concern.

"You're still cold," she murmured.

Before he could respond, she reached out and pressed her palm to his cheek. He could feel the heat of her inner flame radiating through her, seeping into him like sunlight. Dave's breath caught in his throat.

Then she seemed to realize what she had done and started to pull away.

"I'm sorry, I shouldn't have—"

"Don't."

His hand moved before his mind could catch up, covering hers, holding it against his face. Her skin was silk beneath his palm.

"Don't apologize," he said.

Lena stilled. Her gaze lifted to meet his, wide and uncertain. She was so close that he could see the gentle curve of her lower lip, smell the faint, smoky scent of her hair.

His free hand rose to her face, cupping her cheek as she had cupped his. He hesitated, giving her the chance to pull away.

She didn't move.

Dave leaned forward and closed the small distance between them.

Her lips were warm and soft as he gently pressed his mouth to hers. For a moment, Lena went still beneath his touch, but then something in her gave way.

She leaned into him, her lips parting beneath his, her hand sliding from his jaw to the back of his neck. The restraint Dave had been clinging to shattered like ice beneath a hammer. He deepened the kiss, his hand tangling in her locks, pulling her closer until he could feel her body against his.

She let him. More than that, she matched him, her fingers threading through his hair, her breath mingling with his. The cold that had been gnawing at his bones retreated, driven back by her flame, her nearness, the intoxicating reality of her in his arms.

The kiss had not lasted nearly long enough when they parted.

A smile stole onto Dave's lips as he gazed into her eyes.

Lena smiled back.

He shifted on the bed, making room beside him, and drew her gently into his embrace. She came willingly, settling against his side, her head finding the hollow of his shoulder as if it had always belonged there. They sat propped against the pillows together, her body soft and supple against his, the wind still howling beyond the window.

"Will you let me stay a while?" she asked quietly. "I could warm you more. You're still shivering."

"You don't have to—"

"But I want to."

Her words pierced him more deeply than any declaration could have. She *wanted* to. Wanted to be here. With *him.*

"All right," he murmured, turning to press a kiss to her hair.

They lay down together in the narrow bed. Dave stretched out on his back, still wearing his shirt and trousers—propriety hadn't entirely fled him yet. Lena curled against his side, her head resting on his shoulder, one arm draped across his chest. Her palm came to rest directly over his heart.

And then she let her fire flow.

It was nothing like before in the back room. This was gentler, more intimate. A slow, steady pulse of heat that seeped through his shirt and into his skin, spreading through his veins until it reached his very core. Dave sighed as the warmth suffused him, his muscles unknotting, the last tremors of cold fading away.

"That feels..." He couldn't find words adequate to describe it. Her flame was filling the emptiness his magic had carved out of him, restoring something he hadn't realized was missing. "Incredible."

"Good," she murmured, her breath warm on his neck. A shiver ran through him that no longer stemmed from the cold.

Dave let his eyes drift closed. He listened to the wind howling against the shutters and the steady crackle of the stove, finally surrendering to the peace.

After a while, he stirred. "That's enough," he said gently, covering her hand with his own. "You'll exhaust yourself."

"I'm fine."

"Lena."

She sighed but relented, the flow of heat slowly ebbing. Her hand remained where it was, though, pressed flat against his chest. He could feel his own heartbeat beneath her palm, once again strong and steady.

Yet she made no move to separate from him.

As the silence stretched between them, Dave was deeply aware of everywhere their bodies touched: her head on his shoulder, her arm across him, her hip pressed against his side.

"Dave?" Her voice was hesitant, barely above a whisper.

"Yes?"

A pause. Then: "Can I stay with you tonight?"

His heart stuttered. He turned toward her, propping himself on one elbow so he could see her face. Her eyes were wide in the firelight.

Dave raised his hand, cradling her face with a tenderness he hadn't known he possessed.

"Yes," he said.

And then he kissed her.

This time, he didn't hesitate. He claimed her mouth with everything he couldn't say; the loneliness of years spent in isolation, the wonder of finding someone who understood him, the desperate hope that this was real.

Lena answered in kind.

Her hands gripped his shirt, pulling him closer. The kiss deepened as the fire between them built. Dave felt her flame flaring brighter, and the heat of her was the most intoxicating thing he had ever known.

He pulled back just far enough to look at her. "Lena," he said, his voice rough, strained with the effort of holding himself back. "If you want to stop—"

Her gaze was dark, fierce with intent. "I don't want to stop."

The last of his restraint dissolved.

He kissed her again, a feverish, desperate sort of hunger taking over, his hands finding the laces at the back of her dress. She helped him with the fastenings, then fumbled with the buttons of his shirt, and soon their clothes lay discarded on the floor beside the bed.

If any chill remained in the air, Dave didn't feel it. Lena's warmth surrounded him, shielded him against the draft seeping through the walls.

She was breathtaking.

Her skin glowed in the low light, smooth and warm beneath his hands. Her eyes never left his as he lowered himself over her, as his hands traced the curves of her body, the dip of her waist, the swell of her hip, the softness of her inner thigh. She shivered beneath him.

"I've wanted this," he murmured, lifting his head to meet her gaze. "You have no idea how long I've wanted this."

She pulled him closer, her lips finding his, her body arching into his touch.

When his fingers found the heat between her thighs, she gasped, her hips lifting to meet him. She was wet, ready for him, and the realization made his own need spike, sharp and demanding.

He didn't stop there. He parted her folds and pushed two fingers inside. She was incredibly tight, clutching at him, and when he curled his fingers to stroke the sensitive spot within, her head fell back against the pillow with a broken sob.

"Please," she whimpered, her hands clinging to his shoulders. "Dave, please..."

That was all the invitation he needed.

He positioned himself over her, pressing his length against her entrance, meeting her eyes in the dim light—a silent question, a final confirmation.

She answered by wrapping her legs around his waist and pulling him closer.

A raw sound escaped them both as he pushed inside. The friction was so intense that it stole the breath from his lungs. Her body squeezed around him, sheathing him so completely that the sensation was almost overwhelming. Dave held himself still, giving her body time to adjust, watching her face for any sign of discomfort. But she only pulled him deeper, her hips rising to meet his.

"Move," she breathed. "Please, move."

He withdrew and thrust again, adjusting the angle, learning what brought her pleasure. It was a friction of skin against skin, his hardness meeting her softness, her body yielding to accept him.

Lena met him stroke for stroke, her nails digging into his shoulders, urging him faster. Her heat surrounded him, filled him, her inner flame pulsing in time with their joining. Dave felt as though he were being engulfed and renewed all at once, her fire burning away the cold emptiness that had haunted him for so long.

He gave himself over to it. Let her consume him. Let her warmth pour into the parts of him that ached for her.

And in return, he poured his energy into her.

It happened without conscious thought—a pulse of golden light between them, his magic responding to the intensity of their connection. Lena inhaled sharply, her eyes flying wide. His light bled into her fire, feeding it, until the pleasure was a sharp, bright edge between them.

"Dave—" Her voice was breathless, wondering. "What—"

"I don't know." He thrust deeper, harder. "Does it matter?"

"No." She pulled him down for a kiss.

The world outside ceased to exist. There was only this room, the fire in the grate, and the woman beneath him.

Lena's body began to tighten around him, her breath coming in short, ragged bursts, her nails raking down his back.

The pressure at the base of his spine coiled tight, and he held back with sheer force of will. He wanted to feel her shatter first. Needed to know he had brought her to the edge and over it.

"Give yourself to me," he murmured against her throat, his hips driving into her with relentless rhythm. "Let me feel you come undone."

She cried out—a sound of pure, unrestrained pleasure—and he felt her throb around him, her inner walls pulsating, her flame blazing so bright he could feel its heat radiating from her skin. The golden glow of his magic flared in answer, and for one breathless moment they were not two separate beings but one—fire and life force merged, burning together.

His release crashed through him.

He buried himself deep inside her and let go, spilling his light into her fire. The pleasure rolled through him, leaving him shaking and breathless.

When the tremors finally slowed, he didn't have the energy to move. He collapsed beside her, his limbs heavy, gathering her close against him.

They lay tangled together, hearts pounding. The fire in the stove had burned low, but Dave barely noticed. His body was warm now, in a way it hadn't been in a long time.

Lena nestled closer against him, her head finding its place on his shoulder, her arm coming around him.

He pulled the blanket up over them both and held her close, listening to the wind easing outside, feeling her breath even out into the steady rhythm of sleep.

He followed her into slumber moments later, more at peace than he had been in years.

Lena woke slowly, gradually drifting up from the depths of dreamless sleep.

The first thing she became aware of was another body pressed against hers. The weight of an arm across her waist. The slow, even breathing that wasn't her own.

Dave.

Her eyes fluttered open.

Pale winter sunlight streamed through the upper half of the window, painting the small chamber in shades of gold and cream. The lower half of the glass was buried in snow, but where the light came through, it fell across the bed in a bright band, illuminating the man sleeping beside her.

He looked different.

Lena propped herself up, careful not to wake him, and studied his face. The healthy color had returned to his skin. More than that, in fact. He looked vital. Younger than she had ever seen him, as if the night had washed years of weariness away. Even the shadows under his eyes, those faint bruises that had always been present no matter how much he rested, had vanished.

She thought of the golden light that had passed between them. The pulse of his life force flowing into her as her fire flowed into him. Had her magic done this? Had the joining of their gifts somehow healed more than just the cold in his bones?

The memory of the night before washed over her, sending a fresh wave of warmth through her blood.

She remembered the tenderness in his hands, the way he had looked at her, and the moment when that gentleness had given way to hunger. The feeling of him inside her, stretching her with a delicious fullness, and the golden light that had lifted them both.

A soft sound escaped her throat at the memory, and Dave stirred beside her.

His eyes opened slowly—found hers—and lingered there, as though he needed to reassure himself she was real.

Then he smiled. A slow, wondering smile that made her heart stutter.

"Good morning," he said, his voice rough with sleep.

"Good morning." She couldn't help smiling back. "How do you feel?"

He stretched, the motion making the blanket slip down to reveal his bare chest. Lena's eyes followed the movement before she could stop herself.

"Better than I have in years," he admitted. "Maybe ever." He reached up to touch her face, his thumb brushing her cheek. "I think I have you to thank for that."

"I didn't do anything."

"You did everything." His expression grew serious, though the warmth in his eyes remained. "Last night... Lena, I've never experienced anything like that. Whatever happened between us, whatever our magic did when we..." He trailed off, a faint flush coloring his cheeks.

"When we made love?" she supplied.

His flush deepened, but he nodded. "It healed something in me. Something I didn't even know was broken." He pulled her closer, pressing a kiss to her forehead. "Thank you."

Lena nestled against him, her head coming to rest against his chest. "Is there anything that needs doing today? Anything urgent at Haven?"

Dave glanced toward the window, taking in the snow piled halfway up the glass.

"We're snowed in," he said. "Nothing's getting in or out of Haven today. Mrs. Finch will have everything well in hand downstairs." A slow smile curved his lips. "Which means we have nowhere to be."

"Oh?" She tilted her head to look up at him. "And how do you intend to spend this unexpected reprieve?"

His smile darkened. In one smooth motion, he rolled, pulling her with him until she was sprawled across his chest, her hair tumbling around them like a dark curtain.

"I can think of a few ways," he murmured.

Lena laughed—a genuine, joyful sound that surprised even her. When was the last time she had laughed like that? She couldn't remember.

But then their eyes met, and the laughter faded. The air between them grew heavy, charged with a sudden shift in gravity.

Dave raised his head and kissed her.

It started tender, sweet and unhurried. But the tenderness didn't last. Not with the memory of last night still burning in her blood, not with the evidence of his renewed desire pressing insistently against her belly.

The kiss deepened. Grew hungry. His hands slid down her back, pulling her closer, and she felt her fire flare.

She broke the kiss just long enough to meet his eyes. "Staying in bed," she breathed, "sounds absolutely wonderful."

Desire blazed in his gaze. He pulled her down to kiss her again. When his tongue coaxed her lips apart, she sighed into his mouth.

His hands roamed down her body, following the curve of her spine. When his fingers moved lower, slipping beneath the blanket to cup her backside, she inhaled sharply against his mouth.

But she wanted more. Wanted to explore. Wanted to see all of him.

She pulled back, a mischievous impulse taking hold. Before he could protest, she was sliding down his body, trailing kisses along his jaw, his throat, his chest. Her tongue flicked against his nipple, and the hiss of pleasure he made sent a thrill straight to her core.

"Lena—"

She didn't stop. Her mouth continued its descent, kissing down the flat plane of his stomach. When her fingers wrapped around his length, he groaned, his hips jerking beneath her.

"Let me," she murmured, looking up at him through her lashes. "I want to taste you."

The sound he made, low and rough, was answer enough.

She lowered her head and took him in, moving slowly, her tongue swirling around the tip before sliding down, taking him deeper. Her lips tightened around him, her hand stroking what her mouth couldn't reach.

His fingers tangled in her hair, holding on. She found a rhythm that made his breath hitch, made him gasp her name.

"Lena... if you don't stop, I'm going to—"

She pulled back with one final, lingering lick, satisfaction curling through her at the desperate look on his face. Then his hands were on her, hauling her up, and he kissed her hungrily until her head spun.

He rolled them in one fluid motion, and suddenly she was beneath him, his weight pressing her into the mattress in the most delicious way.

"Now let me," he said, his voice rough.

He kissed down her throat, her collarbone, the valley between her breasts. When he took one nipple into his mouth, sucking gently, then harder, she moaned. His hand found her other breast, rolling the stiff peak between his fingers, and she writhed beneath him.

"Dave, please—"

He kissed lower, across her stomach, her hip, the skin of her inner thigh. She was trembling now, her breath coming in short bursts. When he settled between her legs and dragged his tongue through her center, she cried out, her hands fisting in the sheets.

He held her steady and savored her—licking, sucking, teasing. Then he slid two fingers inside her, curling them to find the spot that made her breath catch, his tongue working her sensitive bud in relentless circles.

"I need—Dave, I need you inside me—"

He rose over her, positioning himself at her

threshold, as if he too couldn't bear another moment apart. "Look at me," he said.

Her eyes found his, dark and burning with desire, and he entered her in one smooth thrust. Her lips parted on a ragged exhale, her fingers clutching at his biceps.

He didn't stay there. Instead, he withdrew almost completely, sliding back until he was barely touching her. When she arched off the mattress to chase him, seeking the friction, he held himself just out of reach.

"Tell me what you want," he growled low in his throat. "I need to hear you say it."

"You," she pleaded, desperate to feel him again. "I want all of you."

A rough sound tore from his throat, and he thrust deep, filling her whole. Then he hooked one of her legs over his shoulder, changing the angle, driving to her very core, and she groaned at the new sensation. She threw her head back against the pillow, a deep moan escaping her lips as he increased his pace, each stroke more urgent than the last.

Her fire rose unbidden, and she felt his light kindling to meet it. Golden energy was pulsing between them where their bodies touched.

Her breath came faster, her center clenching around him. He drove relentlessly, chasing the edge with her. His thumb found the swollen bundle of nerves above where they joined, rubbing against the sensitive peak with maddening precision.

"Fall with me," he groaned against her throat.

She came apart.

The climax crashed through her in rhythmic waves, her vision going white at the edges. She heard herself cry out, felt her body contract around him, felt the answering pulse of his release as he buried himself deep and followed her over the edge.

His magic flared bright, mingling with her heat in a blaze of gold and amber, then slowly dimmed, leaving them both trembling.

In the quiet that followed, they lay wrapped in each other, heartbeats slowly settling. Outside, the snow had begun falling again, showing no signs of stopping.

And Lena found herself hoping it never would.

CHAPTER 4

The late summer sun hung low over Greyport, painting the sky in shades of amber and rose. Lena walked through the Warrens with a lightness in her step that would have been unimaginable eight months ago, when she had stumbled through these same streets, half-starved and desperate.

How different everything was now.

She shifted the basket on her arm. It was nearly empty now, save for the glass jars she was bringing back to Mrs. Finch. The rest of its contents—herbal salves, fresh bandages, and half the bread from the kitchen—she had distributed during her rounds. There were always those too proud or too frail to come to the shelter, the old veterans in the alleyways who still bore the scars of the border wars with the Fae, and the families huddled in tenements that had grown old and brittle with neglect. She visited them daily, offering what comfort she could.

But as she moved through the streets, her eyes were always scanning. Noting who was there and who wasn't. Dave's warning about people disappearing still echoed in her mind, and while she couldn't be sure if the absences she noticed were sinister or simply the transient nature of life in the Warrens, she remained alert.

The warm breeze carried the scent of late-blooming flowers from somewhere nearby, mingling with the less pleasant odors of the quarter. But even those didn't bother her anymore. This place had become home in a way she never could have anticipated. These narrow streets, these cramped buildings, these people who nodded and smiled as she passed—they were hers now. Her community. Her purpose.

And waiting for her at Haven, as he did every evening when she returned, was Dave.

She smiled at the thought of him. Six months had passed since that winter storm had trapped them together in his small chamber. Six months since she had offered to help carry his burden.

And he had let her.

He had taught her the delicate art of securing donations without begging, how to navigate the egos of minor lords, and the intricate web of logistics that kept Haven running.

The days were often long and hard, which made the quiet moments they stole together feel all the more precious: the tea she prepared for him in the quiet of dawn before the rest of the house stirred, the way his hand found hers across a cluttered desk, the private smile reserved only for her.

And their nights...

Heat rose to Lena's cheeks. It wasn't just the physical pleasure that made their connection so special, or even the way their magic intertwined until boundaries dissolved. It was the absolute completeness she felt in his arms. Lying tangled with him in the dark, listening to his steady breathing, she would feel so utterly whole that the thought of ever being without him made her chest ache with a quiet, terrifying dread.

The evening sun was slanting through the buildings as Lena turned onto the street that led to Haven. As she rounded the final corner, she spotted a familiar figure sitting on an overturned crate near the entrance, whittling a piece of scrap wood.

Little John. One of Haven's regulars, though he stubbornly refused a bed inside, preferring the freedom of the streets during the warmer months. Still, he never missed a meal. He was fifteen years old, rail-thin, with a shock of red hair that refused to lie flat no matter how much Mrs. Finch tried to tame it.

"Good evening, John," Lena called as she approached.

The young man looked up, his freckled face breaking into a smile. He tucked his knife away and stood to meet her. "Evening, Miss Lena. Fine day, isn't it?"

"Beautiful," she agreed, pausing beside him. "Will you be joining us for supper tonight?"

"Wouldn't miss Mrs. Finch's cooking for nothing. She promised apple tart for pudding. Said she'd save me a double portion if I helped her peel the fruit this morning."

Lena laughed. "And did you?"

"Course I did. My fingers still smell of apples." He held up his hands as proof, grinning.

She was about to respond when a sound caught her ear—the heavy stomp of a hoof against cobblestones, followed by the jingle of a harness.

She turned to look, and frowned.

A carriage stood in front of Haven.

It was sleek and elegant, painted a glossy black that gleamed even in the fading light. The horses that drew it were magnificent creatures, their coats so dark they seemed to absorb the shadows around them. Silver fittings adorned the doors and wheels, catching the last rays of the sun and throwing back cold sparks of light.

It was the most expensive carriage Lena had ever seen. And it was utterly, jarringly out of place in the Warrens.

"John," she said, not taking her eyes off the coach. "Do you know who that belongs to?"

The young man followed her gaze, his expression growing uncertain. "Arrived maybe ten minutes ago, Miss. Driver stayed with the horses, but a gentleman went up to the door. Looked like Dave let him in."

A gentleman. Inside Haven.

A feeling of unease settled in Lena's stomach. The wealthy donors Dave cultivated knew to be discreet. They sent servants with supplies, or arranged meetings in neutral locations. They didn't arrive in ostentatious carriages that announced their presence to the entire neighborhood.

Unless...

The thought struck her with sudden force. The benefactor.

She remembered the conversation she and Dave had shared just a few weeks ago, heads bent over the ledger. She had pressed him again about the mysterious man who funded their work.

"Haven't I proven that you can trust me?" she'd asked. "Haven has become my home. And yet I've never met the man who makes it all possible."

Dave had set down his pen, his expression guarded. "He values his privacy, Lena. When he's ready to reveal himself, he will."

"Even if it means keeping secrets from me?"

"It's not my secret to share."

Lena's grip tightened on her basket. Was this him? Had the mysterious patron finally decided to reveal himself?

"Thank you, John," she said, keeping her voice steady. "I'll see you at supper."

"Yes, Miss." But his eyes lingered on the carriage, and she could see her own wariness reflected in his gaze.

Lena continued toward the shelter, her earlier lightness replaced by a growing tension. As she drew closer, rounding the back of the carriage, the weathered timber door ahead pushed outward. Dave stepped out first, followed by a stranger.

Dave's posture was rigid, his arms crossed over his chest. He wore the expression she had come to recognize as his diplomatic mask—polite, composed, revealing nothing of his true thoughts. But she knew him well enough now to notice the subtle tightness around his jaw.

Something was wrong.

The stranger stood with his back to Lena. He was tall and lean, dressed in impeccably tailored clothes that probably cost more than Haven's entire monthly budget. A top hat sat perfectly positioned on his head, dark hair peppered with silver visible beneath its brim. In one hand he held a cane with a silver tip.

She was too far away to hear what they were saying at first, but she saw Dave shake his head.

"Thank you, but no," she heard him say as she drew closer. "I'm needed here at Haven."

The stranger's response was quiet and cultured, smooth as polished glass. "How disappointing. I had so hoped we might come to an arrangement."

Dave said nothing. Simply stood his ground, his expression unchanging.

The stranger gave a short nod and touched the brim of his hat. "Good evening, then. I do hope we'll meet again."

He turned toward the carriage.

And Lena got her first clear look at his face.

He was handsome. That was her first, unwilling thought. Handsome in a sharp, angular way, with high cheekbones and a strong jaw. Features that might have been carved from marble. Pale blue eyes, cold as a winter sky, were set in a face strangely youthful despite the silver in his hair.

He didn't look like a philanthropist. He looked like a man who was used to owning things.

A confident smile curved his lips as he climbed into the carriage, the door closing behind him with a soft click. The driver snapped the reins and the majestic black horses surged forward.

Lena stood frozen as the carriage rolled away down the narrow street, turning the corner and disappearing from view. Then she shook herself and hurried the last few steps to Haven's entrance, where Dave still stood in the doorway.

"Who was that?" she asked.

Dave's expression shifted when he saw her, his diplomatic mask giving way to a soft, warm smile. But she saw the tension that lingered in his shoulders, the way his jaw remained tight as he reached out to take the basket from her arm.

"No one important," he said. "Just some rich lord."

"What did he want?"

Dave seemed to weigh his words before answering.

"He made me an offer," he said finally, his smile faltering. "I declined."

"Nothing more?"

"Nothing more." He stepped aside to let her enter, one hand coming to rest at the small of her back in a gesture so familiar, so intimate, that it normally would have made her smile. "Nothing to worry about, Lena."

She wanted to believe him. But as she stepped into the hall, she couldn't shake the image of the stranger's smile. It hadn't been the smile of a man who had accepted a refusal.

It had been the smile of a man who enjoyed the chase.

As Dave led Lena into Haven, the main hall was already filling with residents gathering for supper.

He could feel Lena's eyes on him, could sense her holding back. She had always been perceptive. It was one of the things he loved about her, and he knew she hadn't been satisfied by his dismissive answer about the stranger. But before she could press further, Mrs. Finch called out from the back of the hall.

"Lena! There you are, girl. I need an extra pair of hands with the bread. The loaves are burning and Mary's gone and cut her finger again."

Lena hesitated, glancing at Dave.

"Go on," he said, managing a smile. "I need to go through the accounts anyway. I'll see you at supper."

She held his gaze for a beat longer, her eyes full of unasked questions. "We'll talk later?"

"Later," he agreed.

She nodded, pausing only briefly to squeeze his hand before she went.

His gaze followed her until she disappeared into the kitchen. Then he turned and climbed the stairs to his chamber, his easy manner slipping away with each step.

The room was still, the light fading to a dusty gray beyond the window. Dave closed the door behind him and leaned against it, letting out a long, heavy breath.

Then he reached into his back pocket and pulled out the calling card.

It was fine quality, thick cream-colored paper, the edges gilt, the name and address embossed in sharp black lettering. Dave turned it over in his fingers, studying the name he had already committed to memory.

The Lord's offer echoed in his thoughts.

An enormous sum. More money per year than Dave would have dared hope to earn in a lifetime. Enough to feed Haven's residents for decades. Enough to expand, to take in more people, to do more good than he had ever imagined possible.

And the man had made it sound so simple.

Come work for me. I will pay you handsomely, and you will want for nothing.

But the price was his autonomy.

Exclusive service. Dave would belong to him, his time, his abilities, his very person at the man's disposal. He would be housed on the estate, never permitted to leave the premises without explicit permission. A luxurious prison, but a prison nonetheless.

He could never accept such an offer. Not for any amount of money. The people here depended on him. He couldn't abandon them to live as some wealthy lord's kept servant, no matter how handsomely he might be compensated.

Dave crossed to the desk and sat heavily in the chair. He pulled the drawer out until it hit the stops, then lifted out the ledger with the accounts and set it aside. Reaching into the very back of the empty space, his fingers found the almost invisible seam in the wood. He pried up the false bottom to reveal the hiding spot he had crafted years ago to keep a small cache of emergency coin.

There was no coin there now. Just a small velvet box.

He tossed the calling card into the shallow compartment and reached for the box, setting it on the desk before him.

It was simple. Dark blue velvet, worn thin with age. It had belonged to his mother, one of the few things he had salvaged before the creditors had taken everything else.

Dave eased the lid open.

The ring inside caught the fading light. It wasn't a grand jewel, just a small garnet set in a band of worked silver. But it was real, and it was his.

He picked it up, turning it between his fingers. The stone was a deep crimson, matching the smoldering glow in Lena's eyes when she called forth her fire.

It had to be enough.

He had been waiting for the right moment. Searching for the courage to ask her if a life with him—uncertain and modest though it might be— was a life she would choose.

Because he could not bear a life without her.

That was the truer reason why he had refused the stranger's offer. A reason that went beyond duty or pride.

The thought of being separated from her, of waking each morning far from the Warrens, far from the shelter, far from her, made his chest tight.

When had she become so essential to him? He couldn't name the exact moment. Perhaps it had been during that first winter night they had spent together, when she had poured her fire into his frozen body and looked at him, her gaze full of fierce determination. Or perhaps it had been the accumulation of all the small moments since then; the shared meals, the quiet laughter in the chaos of the day, the way she looked at him when she thought he wasn't watching.

It didn't matter when. What mattered was that he loved her.

He had known it for months now, had felt his feelings for her growing stronger with each passing day. But he had been afraid to act on them. Afraid that he had nothing to offer her. No fortune, no title. Just a drafty shelter in the worst part of the city and a life lived in the shadows.

And yet, she had chosen to stay. She had woven herself so thoroughly into the fabric of Haven—and into his heart—that he couldn't imagine a future without her.

Perhaps tomorrow. He would take her to that small park they sometimes visited, the one with the quiet pond. They would sit on their favorite bench as the sun dipped low, stealing a moment of peace. And there, he would ask her.

Mrs. Finch's voice rang up from below, interrupting his thoughts.

"Supper's ready! Come and get it before it goes cold!"

Dave took a steadying breath, his pulse quickening at the thought of the question he intended to ask.

He placed the ring back into its box and dropped it into the hidden compartment with the calling card. Grabbing the false bottom, he pressed it back into place. In his hurry, the wood caught at an angle, letting out a sharp crack as he forced it down.

Dave frowned, running a thumb over the edge. It wasn't sitting quite flat anymore.

There was no time to fix it now. He would deal with it later.

He pushed the drawer shut and stood up, smoothing his shirt.

Tomorrow, he told himself. He would ask her tomorrow.

CHAPTER 5

The door to Dave's chamber clicked shut behind them, sealing out the noise of the shelter below.

Lena turned to face him. She had held her tongue during supper, forcing herself to make polite conversation with the residents while her mind replayed the image of the black carriage over and over. But she couldn't pretend any longer.

"Tell me what really happened," she demanded. "With that man."

Dave sighed, running a hand through his hair. "Lena..."

"Don't." She crossed her arms. "I saw your face when you were talking to him. I saw how tense you were. Who was he?"

Dave moved to the window, staring out at the darkness beyond the glass.

"He's a lord," he said finally. "A wealthy one. He's heard rumors about a man in the Warrens who can...

do what I do. He wanted to hire me."

"And you refused?"

"Of course I refused." He turned back to her, his jaw set. "He wanted me to live on his estate. Exclusively. Never leave the premises without his permission. He wanted to own me, Lena. The way the lords own people like us under the Protection of the Realm Act."

Lena's stomach turned. She knew too well what that life looked like. The captivity dressed up as protection, the servitude disguised as luxury.

"I have a bad feeling about this," she said. "The look in his eyes... he didn't seem like a man who accepts no for an answer."

"He'll find what he wants somewhere else." Dave crossed the room to her, taking her hands in his. "He'll move on and forget all about Haven."

"You don't know that."

"No," he admitted, squeezing her hands. "But I won't let him anywhere near us, Lena. I promise."

She wanted to argue, wanted to make him acknowledge the danger she felt in her gut. But the conviction in his voice stopped her.

She stepped into his embrace, pressing her face

against his chest. His arms came around her, holding her close, and she breathed in the familiar scent of him.

"I just don't want to lose this," she murmured against his shirt. "What we have."

"You won't." His lips brushed the top of her head. "I promise."

They stood in silence. Then Dave drew back slightly, and Lena glanced up to find him watching her with an unusual intensity.

"Dave, is everything all right?" she asked.

"Yes." He hesitated, his hands still resting on her waist. "It's just... I was wondering if you would accompany me tomorrow. For a walk."

She blinked, surprised by the sudden change of subject. "A walk?"

"To our place. The park with the pond." He cleared his throat, looking suddenly boyish. "The leaves are just starting to turn. We haven't been there in so long, and I thought..." He trailed off.

A smile tugged at her lips. Whatever had him so flustered, it was endearing. "Of course I'll accompany you. I'd like that."

Relief washed over his face. "Good. That's...

good."

"Dave." She reached up to cup his cheek. "What has come over you? You're acting very strangely."

He caught her hand and pressed a kiss to her palm. "Nothing has come over me. I just want to spend time with you. Is that so surprising?"

"We spend every day together."

"Not like this. Not just the two of us, away from Haven, away from responsibilities." His eyes met hers, warm and intent. "I want to give you a perfect afternoon, Lena. Will you let me?"

There was an edge to his voice, but before she could examine it too closely, he was kissing her. She leaned into him, meeting his lips with a hunger that matched his own. Her fingers curled into the fabric of his shirt as his hands slid up her back, one tangling in her hair, the other pulling her flush against him.

"I want you," he murmured against her lips.

"Then I'm yours," she whispered back.

His fingers found the laces at the back of her dress, tugging them loose with sudden urgency. The dress dropped to the floor. He drew the shift over her head and tossed it aside, then lifted her into his arms and carried her the few steps to the bed, lay-ing her down on the worn quilt.

He shed his own clothes—shirt and trousers discarded in a heap—and settled over her, pressing her into the mattress.

Bracing himself on one elbow, his mouth found her throat, her collarbone, the swell of her breast. Lena tangled her fingers in his hair, hold-ing him there as he grazed his teeth over her hard peak, sending shivers through her. Her free hand roamed the span of his back, sensing his muscles tense be-neath her touch.

Dave slid his hand down her body, over her waist, along the curve of her hip, before moving lower, guiding himself to her threshold.

He sank into her, finding a rhythm that start-ed slow and deep, winding the tension in her lower belly tighter with every stroke. Lena wrapped her legs around his waist, rising to meet him, her move-ments just as demanding as his. Her magic flared to fuse with his, answering the pulse of his light where their bodies joined.

Dave groaned her name, burying his face against her neck. She arched into him, pulling him deeper, and felt the moment his control shattered.

The release crashed through them both, blazing hot and bright, leaving them trembling in its wake.

He collapsed against her, half-draped over her body. Too spent to move—not that she wanted to—Lena let herself drift, grounded by the solid weight of him. Sleep was already pulling her under when she felt Dave shift beside her.

"Lena..."

She turned to face him.

He swallowed, his gaze lingering on her face. Then he leaned over and kissed her forehead.

"Sleep well," he whispered.

Lena smiled, burying her face in the crook of his neck. She knew what he had wanted to say. She wanted to say the same. But she could wait until he was ready.

"Goodnight, Dave," she murmured.

The light in the room was soft, a pale gold that promised a fair day. Dave was already awake, lying on his side and watching Lena sleep, her dark hair scattered across the pillow.

His gaze drifted to the desk across the room. Specifically, to the drawer where the ring waited. By tonight, if all went well, it would be on Lena's finger.

Reaching out, he gently tucked a strand of hair behind her ear. Her skin was warm beneath his fingertips. Always warm.

She stirred at his touch, her brow furrowing before her eyes fluttered open. A slow smile spread across her face as her gaze landed on him.

"Good morning," she murmured.

"Morning," he whispered, leaning down to kiss her.

It started as a gentle greeting, but Lena hummed against his lips and pulled him closer. She was warm and soft beneath the thin sheet, and Dave felt his good intentions slipping. His hand found her waist, tracing the slope of her hip and pulling her against the hard line of his body.

"Breakfast! Everyone to the table!"

Mrs. Finch's voice rang up from below, accompanied by the clatter of pots.

Dave groaned and buried his face in the curve of her shoulder.

"Impeccable timing, as always," he muttered.

Lena laughed, the sound vibrating through her chest. "We should get up."

"Must we?" He looked at her, putting on a pitiful expression. "I find myself hungry for something other than porridge."

"Dave." She pushed gently at his chest, though a smile betrayed her stern tone. "The residents need feeding. And I have my rounds to do."

Dave threw himself back against the pillows with a dramatic sigh. "The cruelty. The absolute cruelty of it all."

Lena laughed again. She squirmed free of his grasp, taking the sheet with her as she sat up. Reaching down, she retrieved his shirt from the floor and threw it at his face. "Get dressed, you ridiculous man."

He caught the garment and stood up, watching as she gathered her own clothes from where they had been discarded the night before. Even with her hair in disarray and traces of sleep still evident in her features, she was breathtaking.

She caught him staring and raised an eyebrow. "What?"

"Nothing." He pulled the shirt over his head. "Just thinking about how lucky I am."

Her expression softened. She crossed to him, rising on her toes to press a kiss to his cheek. "I'm the lucky one."

They dressed quickly, stealing kisses between the buttoning of shirts and the lacing of stays. By the time they were both presentable, Dave had lost count of how many times his lips had found hers.

He didn't mind. He planned to spend the rest of his life losing count.

Breakfast passed in a blur. Mrs. Finch was shouting orders while the residents chatted over their bowls of porridge. Dave sat beside Lena, their shoulders brushing, their hands finding each other beneath the table.

Then, a sharp knock at the front door broke the moment.

Dave stood to answer it, returning a moment later with a folded note in his hand, his brow furrowed.

"Everything all right?" Lena asked.

"A meeting request. Someone wants to discuss a potential donation." He turned the paper over; it was plain, cheap stock. "No name. Just a time and place. Near the old mill, midday."

"Anonymous?" Lena's expression grew dark. "Another one of your secretive donors?"

Dave winced at the edge in her voice. He knew the incident with the Lord yesterday had left her rattled.

"Lena, I genuinely don't know who this is. The note doesn't say."

"And yet you're going?"

"We need the funds," he said, keeping his voice low so the residents wouldn't hear. "Winter is coming. The roof in the west dormitory won't survive another heavy snowfall without repairs. I can't afford to turn down a potential donor, even a shy one."

She was silent for a moment, searching his face. But then she sighed.

"I'm sorry. I just... I worry."

"I know." He covered her hand with his. "Will you still meet me at the park today? After your rounds?" The question came out more tentative than he intended. "I'll be waiting for you at our usual place."

"Of course." She managed a smile, though her expression remained wary.

After they'd finished eating and Lena had gathered her basket, Dave walked her to the door.

The morning was bright, the sky a piercing blue. Dave stepped out onto the stoop with her, reluctant to let her go just yet.

"Be careful out there," he said.

"You too," she replied.

He caught her hand before she could turn away, bringing her knuckles to his lips. He looked at her, the words I love you resting on the tip of his tongue. He wanted to say them. He wanted to shout them.

But not here. Not on a doorstep in the Warrens. He would say them properly tonight, when the ring was on her finger.

"I'll see you at the park," he said instead.

"At the park." She leaned in, pressing a quick, sweet kiss to his cheek. Then she turned and started down the street.

Dave watched until she turned the corner and disappeared from view. Once she was gone, he went back inside and climbed the stairs.

At the desk, he pulled the drawer open. Reaching to the back, his fingers found the edge of the false bottom. It stuck slightly. The wood was warped where he had forced it down last night, but with a little wiggle, it popped loose.

Inside lay the calling card and the velvet box.

He lifted the box out. It was too bulky to hide in his pocket without creating a noticeable lump, so he opened the lid and removed the ring.

Slipping the garnet band into his breast pocket, he patted it once to make sure it was secure. The empty box went back into the hidden compartment.

When he pressed the false bottom back down, it refused to sit even. The corner stuck up noticeably now, but he didn't care. He was going to propose to-day. After that, there would be no more need for hiding spots.

Dave pushed the drawer shut and grabbed his coat.

Today, he thought as he headed for the door. *To-day will be the perfect day.*

The ducks were diving for their supper.

Lena watched them from where she sat on the weathered bench, their feathered bottoms bobbing above the water as they searched for food beneath the surface. A pair of swans glided past, regal and unhurried, leaving gentle ripples in their wake.

The park was quiet at this hour. A few couples were strolling past, arm in arm, an elderly gentle-man was feeding breadcrumbs to the birds, and a governess was shepherding her young charges to-ward the gate. They nodded politely as they passed, and Lena nodded back, touched by the civility of it.

The day's last sun spilled across the rooftops, bathing everything in amber. The leaves on the willows had just begun to turn, their edges tinged with gold and russet. A warm breeze carried the scent of late-blooming roses from somewhere nearby.

It was, she thought, a perfect day.

Her rounds had gone well. She had tended to the fevered, distributed provisions, and directed a few new faces toward Haven. Now she sat on the edge of the bench, smoothing wrinkles from her skirt where there were none as her eyes darted toward the park entrance for the tenth time.

Dave had seemed so eager this morning. So strangely excited about their meeting here. She smiled at the memory of his nervous energy, the way he'd told her he'd be waiting for her.

Waiting for her.

But where was he?

She glanced toward the park entrance, expecting to see his familiar figure striding toward her any moment.

The path remained empty.

She frowned. Dave was never late. His meetings with donors usually ended well before this hour, and he always kept his promises. Always.

The encounter with the lord flickered through her mind; that glossy black carriage, those cold pale eyes, that confident smile.

An uneasy feeling stirred in her stomach.

She pushed it aside. Dave had refused the offer. The man would find what he wanted elsewhere. There was nothing to worry about.

The sun dipped lower.

The park gradually emptied around her, and even the swans retreated to the far side of the pond, settling among the reeds.

Still no Dave.

The unease in her stomach sharpened into something colder as dusk crept across the park, lengthening shadows and chasing the warmth from the air.

Lena stood.

Her walk toward the gate quickened to a stride, then broke into a run. The flutter in her chest had become a pounding, her breath coming faster, her hands trembling at her sides.

Something is wrong.

Her lungs were burning by the time she reached the Warrens, her skirts bunched in her fists, her pulse thundering in her ears. The streets blurred past—familiar corners, familiar faces turning to stare—but she didn't stop, didn't slow until she reached Haven.

She burst inside.

The door flew open with a bang that echoed through the main hall. Every head turned. Spoons froze halfway to mouths. Conversations died mid-sentence.

Mrs. Finch stood behind the serving table, a ladle suspended over the steaming pot. Her eyes went wide at the sight of Lena in the doorway, chest heaving, face pale.

"My dear, what on earth—"

"Dave." His name came out ragged, desperate. "Where is he?"

Mrs. Finch's brow furrowed. "He said he was going to meet you at the park after his engagements today." She lowered the ladle, concern deepening the lines around her eyes. "Is he not with you?"

"No." She shook her head. "He never came."

A hush fell over the hall. Then a young voice spoke up from one of the tables.

"Maybe he got held up talking to that lord again,

Miss Lena?"

She turned. Little John sat hunched over his bowl, his freckled face uncertain.

"I saw the carriage again today. That shiny black one." He swallowed. "It was in the Warrens this afternoon. Near the old mill."

Lena's stomach sank.

She didn't wait to hear more. She turned and took the stairs two at a time, her mind racing. Dave kept meticulous records of his meetings. If that lord had given him a name, an address—anything—it would be in the accounting journal.

She burst into his chamber and went straight to the desk, yanking open the drawer.

As she pulled out the heavy ledger, something caught her eye. She set the book down on the tabletop and leaned closer to inspect the empty compartment.

The bottom of the drawer looked different. One corner of the wood was sticking up, not sitting quite right against the side.

Lena's heart hammered against her ribs. She dug her fingernails under the raised edge and lifted the false bottom out.

Inside lay two objects. A calling card. And a small box, dark blue with hinges at the back.

A ring box.

She lifted it out, her fingers suddenly unsteady. The velvet was soft against her palm, and she hesitated, almost afraid to open it.

Then she lifted the lid.

Empty.

The white satin interior stared back at her, a small indent where a ring had once rested.

She gazed at it, her mind struggling to piece together what this meant.

And then it hit her.

That's why he was so nervous this morning. That's why he wanted to meet her at the park, at their special place, just the two of them. He wasn't just planning an afternoon walk.

He was going to propose.

Her throat ached. She had doubted him. Had questioned his secrecy, his reasons, his trust in her. When in truth, he had been planning to make her his wife.

Her vision blurred.

If he took the ring with him, if he left Haven with

every intention of asking her to marry him, then nothing in this world would have kept him from meeting her.

Unless he couldn't.

She set the empty box down on the desk with trembling hands. Her gaze fell on the other object lying in the hidden space.

The calling card.

She picked it up. It was fine paper with elegant writing, and in the corner, a sigil she recognized instantly: the same one that had adorned the carriage door yesterday. The same carriage John had seen prowling the Warrens today.

Her veins ran cold.

She couldn't move. Couldn't breathe. The card trembled in her grip as the full weight of understanding settled over her.

He had refused. He had said no. And this man had taken him anyway.

Her hands flared hot, the fire rising before she could stop it.

She closed her fingers around the card, crushing it in her fist, then turned and walked out of the room.

Down the stairs. Through the main hall. Past the stunned faces of the residents, past Mrs. Finch who was hurrying toward her with a worried face.

"Lena! What happened? Where are you going?"

Lena didn't stop. Didn't turn. Her eyes fixed straight ahead, her steps steady and sure, her jaw set like iron.

"I am going to see the Marquis."

—To be continued—

Epilogue

The newspaper lay spread across the mahogany desk, its headlines bold in the lamplight.

HARBOR INFERNO CLAIMS 43 LIVES

FIRE STARTER ARRESTED — STORM CALLER SOUGHT FOR QUESTIONING

TWELVE SHIPS DESTROYED IN GREYPORT'S DEADLIEST BLAZE

The young man behind the desk read the words for the third time, his steel-gray eyes dark with exhaustion. The fire in the hearth had burned low, casting the room in shadow, but he made no move to stoke it.

A knock broke the silence. He didn't look up. "Come in."

The door opened to admit a tall figure with golden-blond hair and green eyes, his clothes immaculate despite the hour. The late-night guest crossed the room and dropped into the chair across from the desk without waiting for an invitation.

"You look terrible."

"Thank you for that observation." The man with the gray eyes folded the newspaper and shoved it aside. "I take it you've heard."

"All of Greyport has heard. Forty-three dead. A dozen ships burned to ashes." His friend leaned back, crossing one ankle over his knee. "The taverns are calling it the worst disaster in a generation. And the broadsheets are seizing upon it—'magic users run rampant,' 'Sparks show their true colors.' The usual hysteria."

"It will only get worse." The words came out flat. "The Reform Act has been losing support for years. This will be the excuse the King's Council needs to tighten restrictions. They will enforce registration, impose new limitations, breed fear until the people demand an amendment."

A pause. The visitor's expression sobered, his posture straightening. "The official account claims they acted together. A coordinated attack."

"The papers print whatever sells. Truth be damned."

The young lord rose from his chair and moved to the window, gazing out at the city. Smoke was still rising from the ruined harbor, blotting out the stars. Somewhere out there, a woman sat in a cell awaiting trial for murder, while another ran for her life.

And deep in the shadows of Greyport, a man had vanished without a trace.

"There's something else." His voice was quiet. "David is missing."

The other man straightened. "The one who runs the shelter? Your—"

"Yes." The word cut off whatever descriptor had been coming. "He didn't come to our last scheduled meeting. I sent someone to investigate." He paused, his jaw tightening. "They returned with news that David has been missing for days. Along with the woman who helped him run the shelter."

"You think it's connected?"

"I think too many magic users have been disappearing lately for this to be coincidence." He turned from the window. In the dim light, his face was hard. "I've been tracking the pattern for months. They vanish from the streets, from the shelters, from their homes. Men, women, children—gone."

"And now David."

"And now David."

The only sound in the room was the dying crackle of the fire.

"What do you think really happened?" his friend asked at last. "At the harbor?"

The young earl looked back toward the smoke rising over the city.

"I don't know," he admitted. "But I intend to find out."

ENJOYED *STOLEN HEART*?

Thank you so much for reading. As an independent author, I don't have a big marketing machine behind me—I have you.

If you enjoyed this story, please consider leaving a short review. It takes only a minute, but it makes a huge difference in helping other readers find this world.

Thank you for your support! ♥

Scan to review on Amazon:

(Or find Stolen Heart on Goodreads)

A Brief History of Elthera

Long ago, magic flowed freely through the Kingdom of Elthera. Those born with gifts—fire starters, healers, storm callers, and others—were valued members of society, serving as advisors, protectors, and pillars of their communities.

But magic does not breed true. Over generations, the gifts became rarer, skipping bloodlines, appearing unpredictably. What was once common became exceptional, and what was exceptional became envied. Fear followed envy, as it so often does.

The Church spoke first against the gifted, declaring their abilities unholy. The common people, already uneasy, found permission for their fear in holy doctrine. The witch hunts began.

It was a dark time. Magic users were burned, drowned, hanged. Entire families fled to the wild Northern Reaches or sought refuge in the Western

Planes, where the Fae held sway. Those who remained in the Eastern Territories lived in hiding or died in flames.

In 1742, King Edmund IV faced a choice: allow the extermination to continue, or find another way. His solution pleased no one and satisfied no one. The Containment Decree declared magic users less than human—property to be owned, controlled, and contained. They would not be killed, but neither would they be free. Assigned to noble families as servants and slaves, they became assets to be registered, traded, and inherited—their abilities monitored, their powers used only at their master's command.

For over a century, this was the law of the land.

Then came the Protection of the Realm Act of 1847. King Eldric VII, the present monarch, found the old ways barbaric. Under his reform, magic users were recognized as human once more. Masters could grant freedom. Harassment of the freed became punishable by law.

But freedom, as many discovered, is not the same as equality.

Freed magic users cannot, by law, own property. Cannot run businesses. Cannot testify against their betters in court. They are human in name, but not in right. Many choose to remain in service—at least a noble household offers food, shelter, and a measure of protection. Those who venture out alone find only hunger, hatred, and streets that offer no welcome to their kind.

The faint glow in their eyes marks them—an ethereal shimmer that brightens when their power stirs. The slurs follow: Demons. Cursed. Devil-touched.

Twelve years after the Reform, tensions simmer beneath Elthera's polished surface. There are whispers of magic users disappearing without explanation. The old envy stirs once more, and there are those who seek to claim by force what nature did not grant them. And in the shadows of Greyport's Warrens, small acts of resistance flicker like candle flames against the dark.

The law may have changed.

The hatred has not.

Magic Users of Elthera

The gifted fall into two broad categories:

Elementalists
Those who manipulate matter

- Fire Starter — Commands flame; immune to burning and cold
- Storm Caller — Controls weather, wind, and lightning
- Stone Shaper — Mends and manipulates stone and crystal
- Tide Weaver — Commands water in all its forms

Mentalists
Those who manipulate mind and energy

- Telepath — Reads thoughts and emotions
- Shield — Creates barriers against magical interference (extremely rare)
- Life Force Enhancer — Transfers vital life force energy to others
- Healer — Mends wounds and cures ailments through touch
- And others, rarer still

Discover how the story continues in:

SILENT HEART

The Earl Who Stole Her Thoughts

Sign up for my newsletter
for an exclusive first look at *Silent Heart*,
Book One in the *Tales of Elthera* series.

ABOUT THE AUTHOR

Kaelis Knight's love affair with romance began at thirteen, when she discovered her mother's collection of paperbacks and devoured them in secret. That summer ignited a passion that never faded — guiding her first to a career translating romance novels for a major publisher, and eventually to writing stories of her own.

After years of carefully shaping other authors' words into new languages, Kaelis found that her own characters had begun to whisper. Her own worlds demanded to be built. Her own love stories refused to stay quiet.

Now she writes gaslamp fantasy romance — stories set in worlds of Victorian elegance and forbidden magic, where love builds slowly and burns bright. She writes for readers who stay up too late turning pages, and for everyone who believes that love is the most powerful magic of all.

When she isn't writing, Kaelis enjoys playing guitar, painting, and losing herself in a good book.

Visit **kaelisknight.com** for more.

Newsletter:

kaelisknight.com/newsletter